DUCKS, DUCKS, DUCKS

by Carolyn Otto
pictures by Molly Coxe

HarperCollins*Publishers*

To Father, to Mother,
to my two brothers
—CBO

The art for this book was prepared
using black colored pencil and watercolors.

DUCKS, DUCKS, DUCKS
Text copyright © 1991 by Carolyn B. Otto
Illustrations copyright © 1991 by Molly Coxe
Printed in the U.S.A. All rights reserved.
1 2 3 4 5 6 7 8 9 10
First Edition

Library of Congress Cataloging-in-Publication Data
Otto, Carolyn.
    Ducks, ducks, ducks / by Carolyn Otto ; pictures by Molly Coxe.
        p.   cm.
    Summary: Four young ducks from the country have an exciting
time when they visit their relatives in the city.
    ISBN 0-06-024637-5. — ISBN 0-06-024639-1 (lib. bdg.)
    [1. Ducks—Fiction.   2. City and town life—Fiction.   3. Stories
in rhyme.] I. Coxe, Molly, ill. II. Title.
PZ8.3.O84Du   1991   90-42089
[E]—dc20   CIP
                                                             AC

DUCKS, DUCKS, DUCKS

ducks fast asleep

ducks half awake
ducks in the morning

ducks on the lake

dipping ducks
dripping ducks
dunking
　　ducking
　　　duckling
　　　　ducks

duck sisters
duck brothers

duck fathers
duck mothers

ducks dressed up
ducks dressed down
ducks in the country

ducks in town

duck cars
duck planes
duck trucks
duck trains

walking ducks
waddling ducks
wigging
wagging
wobbling
ducks

ducks in front
ducks behind
ducks every which way
ducks in a line

ducks eating lunch
duck afternoons

ducks at the movies
duck cartoons

ducks in restaurants
ducks at home
ducks watching TV
ducks on the phone

ducks in the evening
ducks at night

ducks in bed
ducks good night